MCR

Items should be returned to a library by closing
time on or before the date stamped above,
unless a renewal has been granted.

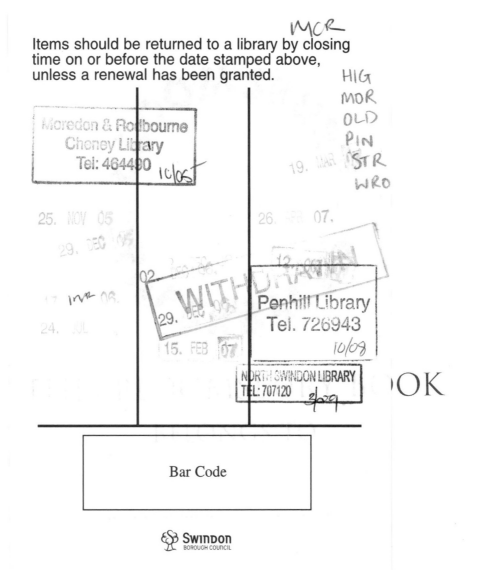

OK

Bar Code

Swindon
BOROUGH COUNCIL

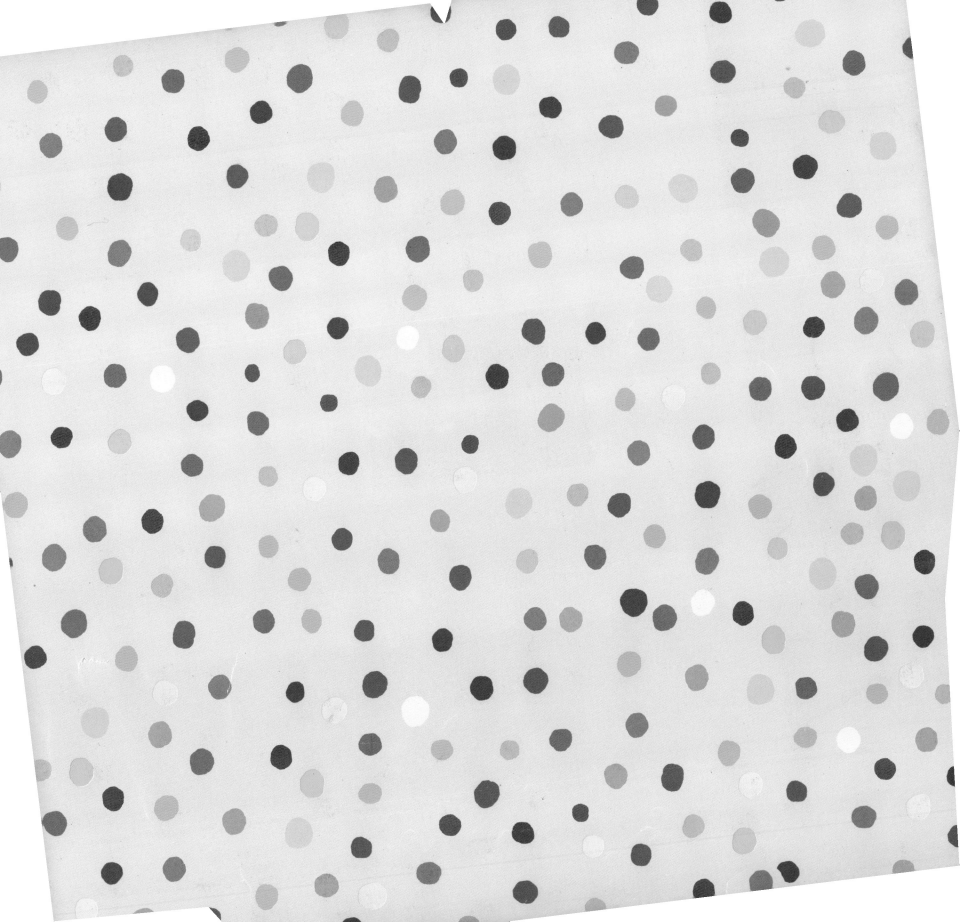

To Ben Brown with love from MMC

BLOOMSBURY
CHILDREN'S
BOOKS

First published in Great Britain in 2005 by Bloomsbury Publishing Plc
38 Soho Square, London, W1D 3HB

A CIP catalogue record of this book is available from the British Library
ISBN 0 7475 5665 2

Designed by Sarah Hodder
Printed and bound by South China Printing Co.

1 3 5 7 9 10 8 6 4 2

All papers used by Bloomsbury Publishing are natural, recyclable products
made from wood grown in well-managed forests. The manufacturing processes
conform to the environmental regulations of the country of origin.

A Big Kiss for Alice

Sally Grindley

illustrated by

Margaret Chamberlain

BLOOMSBURY
CHILDREN'S
BOOKS

'It's your big day tomorrow,' said Dad.
Alice hid under the covers.
'Don't worry,' said Dad. 'Tom will look after you.'

In his bedroom, Tom kicked at his school shoes lying on the floor and threw himself on the bed. Why did his sister always have to spoil things?

Dad came in and sat next to him.
'It won't be as bad as you think,' said Dad.
Tom wriggled uncomfortably and turned away.
'I hope you'll be kind,' said Dad.

In the morning, Alice stood by the front door, clutching her teddy.

'You can't take that stupid thing,' snarled Tom. 'Everyone will laugh at you.'

'You mean you're worried they'll laugh at you, Tom,' Dad said, gently.

Tom went very quiet.

In the car, Alice chatted excitedly. 'Teddy's coming with me because he'll be lonely at home.'

'Tom took Hoppit the Frog,' said Dad. 'He wouldn't be parted from it.'

When they stopped outside the school, Dad put an arm around Tom and said, 'Please keep an eye on Alice. It's a big day for her.'

'It's a horrid day for me,' cried Tom, and he dashed away.

'William play with me?' asked Alice, as Dad took her to her teacher.

'I think you'll want to play with your new friends,' said Dad.

'I don't think Tom likes me,' said Alice.

Tom sat in his classroom and gazed out of the window. A crocodile of first years waddled across the playground. He looked for Alice. Her blond curls bobbed up and down in the middle of the line.

'Which one's your sister?' whispered a friend.

'Who cares?' hissed Tom, and went back to his reading.

At lunchtime, Alice came rushing over to them. 'Teddy likes it here. He wants to come again tomorrow.'

Tom went bright red.

'You and your stupid teddy,' he growled.

Alice's eyes filled with tears.

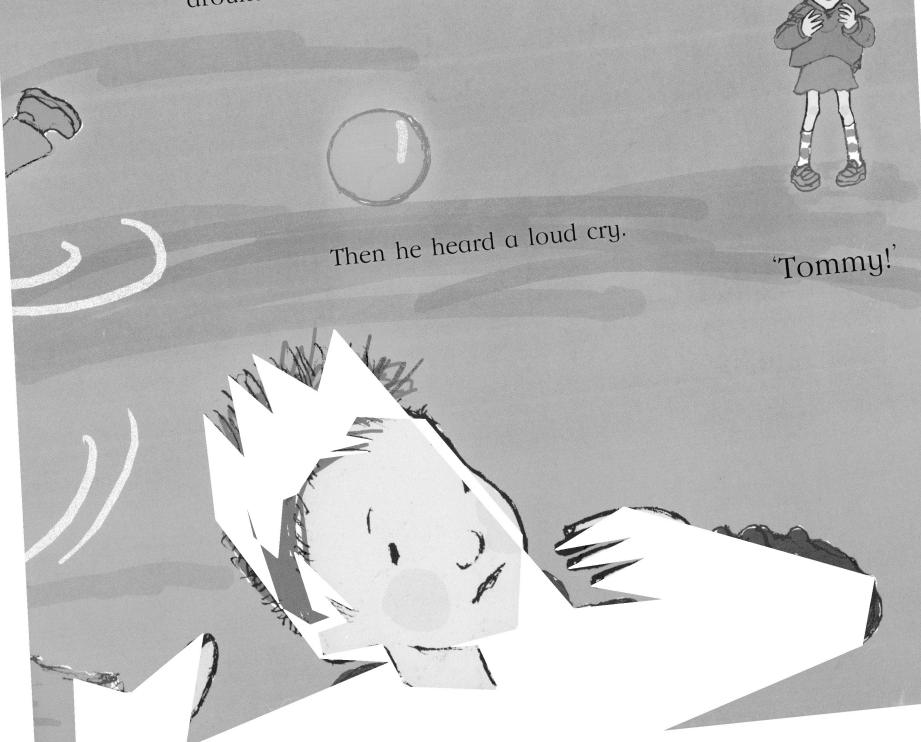

At playtime, Tom kicked a ball and played tag with friends. But he couldn't help looking around to see what Alice was doing.

Then he heard a loud cry.

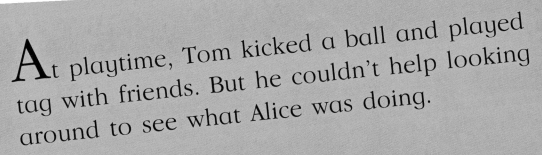

'Tommy!'

Tom sprinted across the playground.
He caught hold of a little boy's arm and
said, gently, 'I think that's Alice's teddy.
Shall I give it back to her?'

The little boy nodded.
Alice wiped away her tears and hugged her teddy tight.
Then Tom gave her a great big kiss, right on the side of
her cheek, and ran away.

When Dad came to collect them, before he could ask how the big day had gone, Alice jumped into his arms and cried, 'Tommy gave me a great big kiss, didn't you Tommy?'

Tom growled and threw himself into the car, but a smile tugged at the corners of his mouth and Dad saw it.

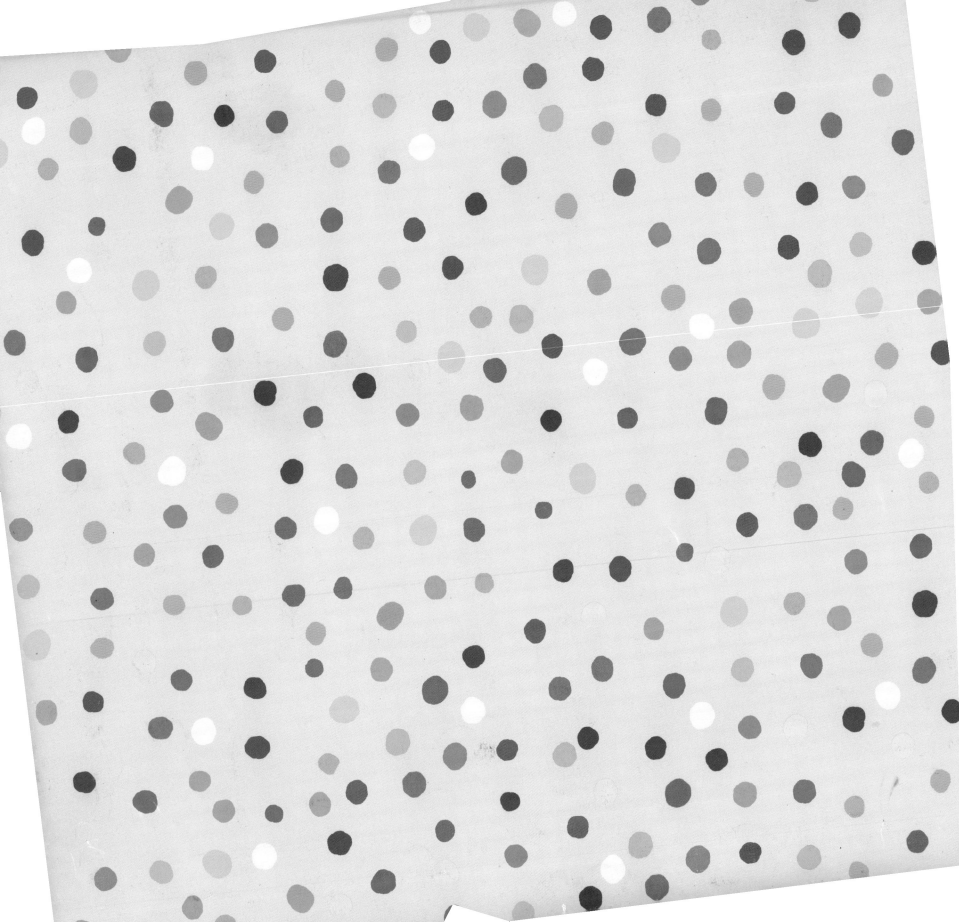

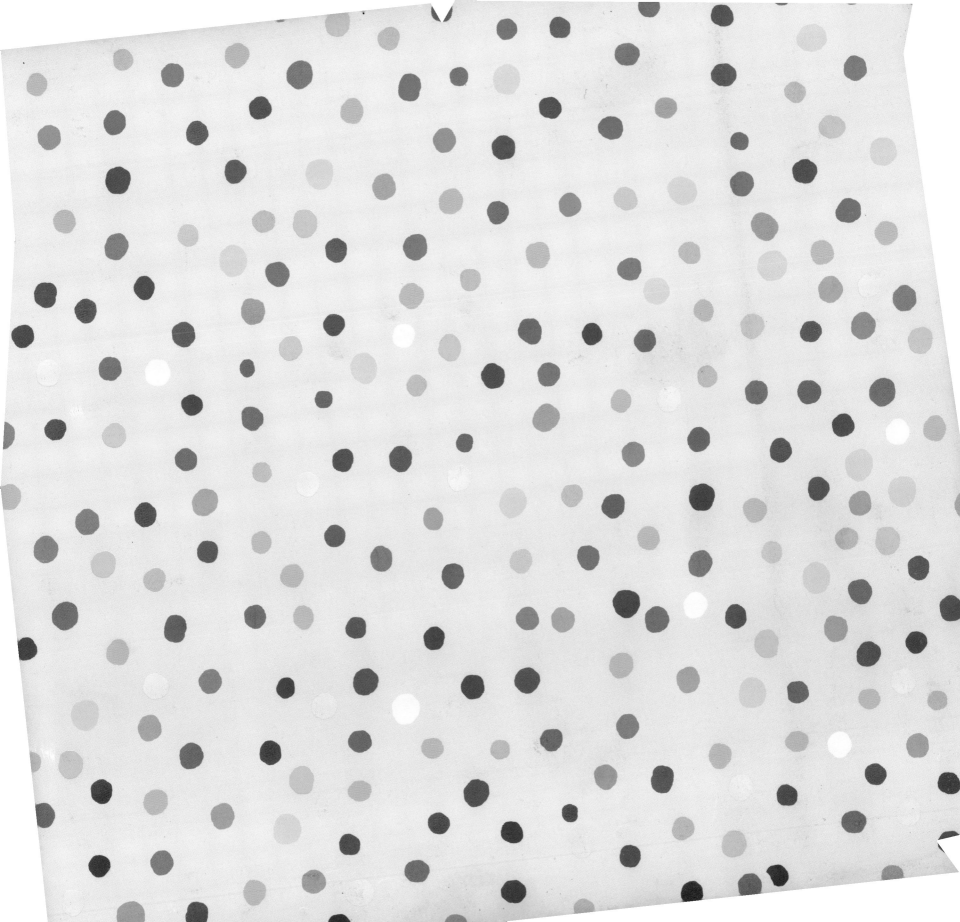

'Sally Grindley excels in stories that extend a child's emotional experience without becoming sentimental or precious' *Scotsman*

Enjoy more great Bloomsbury picture books from Sally Grindley ...

Who Is It?
Sally Grindley and Rosalind Beardshaw

No Trouble At All
Sally Grindley and Eleanor Taylor

A Little Bit of Trouble
Sally Grindley and Eleanor Taylor

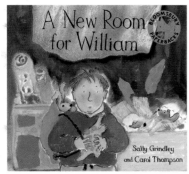

A New Room for William
Sally Grindley and Carol Thompson

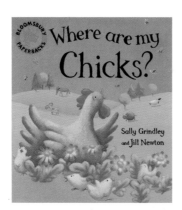

Where Are My Chicks?
Sally Grindley and Jill Newton

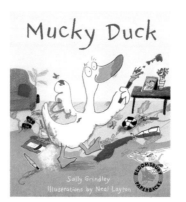

Mucky Duck
Sally Grindley and Neal Layton

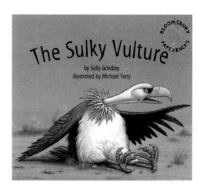

The Sulky Vulture
Sally Grindley and Michael Terry

All available in paperback